To all adopted dogs and the humans they've rescued. To my family.—E.S.O.

For Mom and Dad, who gave me my first pencil.—N.H.

G. P. PUTNAM'S SONS
an imprint of Penguin Random House LLC
375 Hudson Street, New York, NY 10014

G. P. Putnam's Sons is a registered trademark
of Penguin Random House LLC.

Library of Congress Cataloging-in-Publication Data
is available upon request.

Manufactured in China by
RR Donnelley Asia Printing Solutions Ltd.
ISBN 9780399546525
1 2 3 4 5 6 7 8 9 10

Design by Dave Kopka.
Text set in Gotham Rounded.
The art was done in watercolor
and colored pencil.

WALK Your Dog

words by
Elizabeth Stevens Omlor

pictures by
Neesha Hudson

G. P. PUTNAM'S SONS

Greet your dog.

Groom your dog.

Feed your dog.

Dress your dog.

Walk your dog.

Chase your dog.

Catch your dog.

Train

your

dog.

Treat your dog.

Clean your dog.

Settle your dog.

Love your dog.

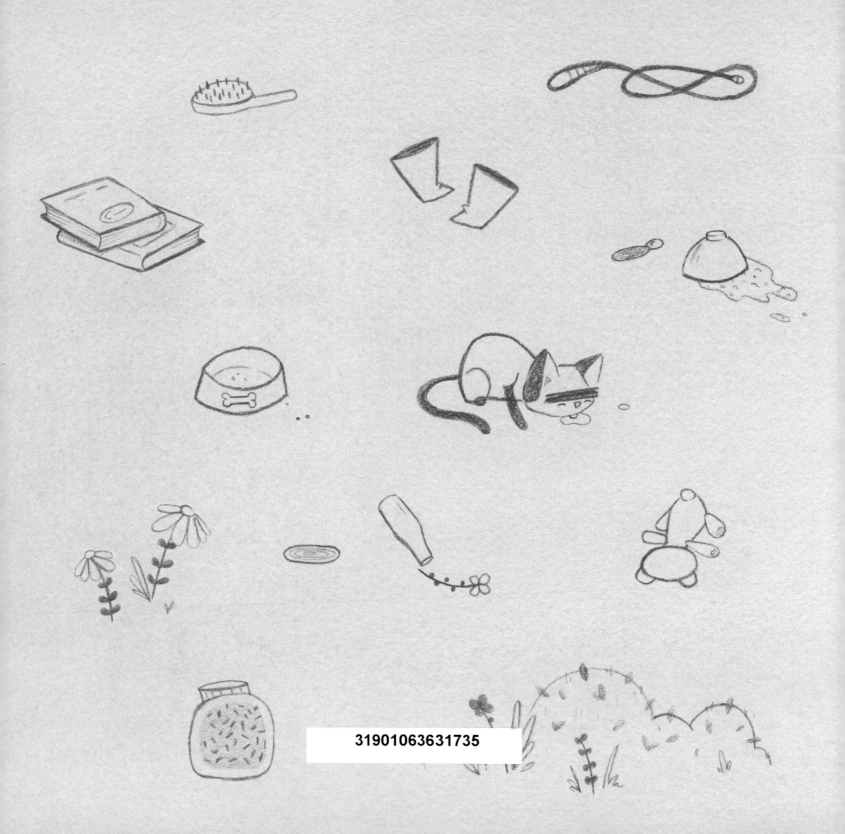